This book belongs to

_____

This book is dedicated to my children - Mikey, Kobe, and Jojo.

Copyright © 2024 Grow Grit Press LLC. All rights reserved. No part of this book may be reproduced in any form without permission in writing from the publisher. Please send bulk order requests to info@ninjalifehacks.tv

Paperback ISBN: 978-1-63731-891-1
Hardcover ISBN: 978-1-63731-893-5
eBook ISBN: 978-1-63731-892-8

Printed and bound in the USA.
NinjaLifeHacks.tv

Ninja Life Hacks®
by Mary Nhin

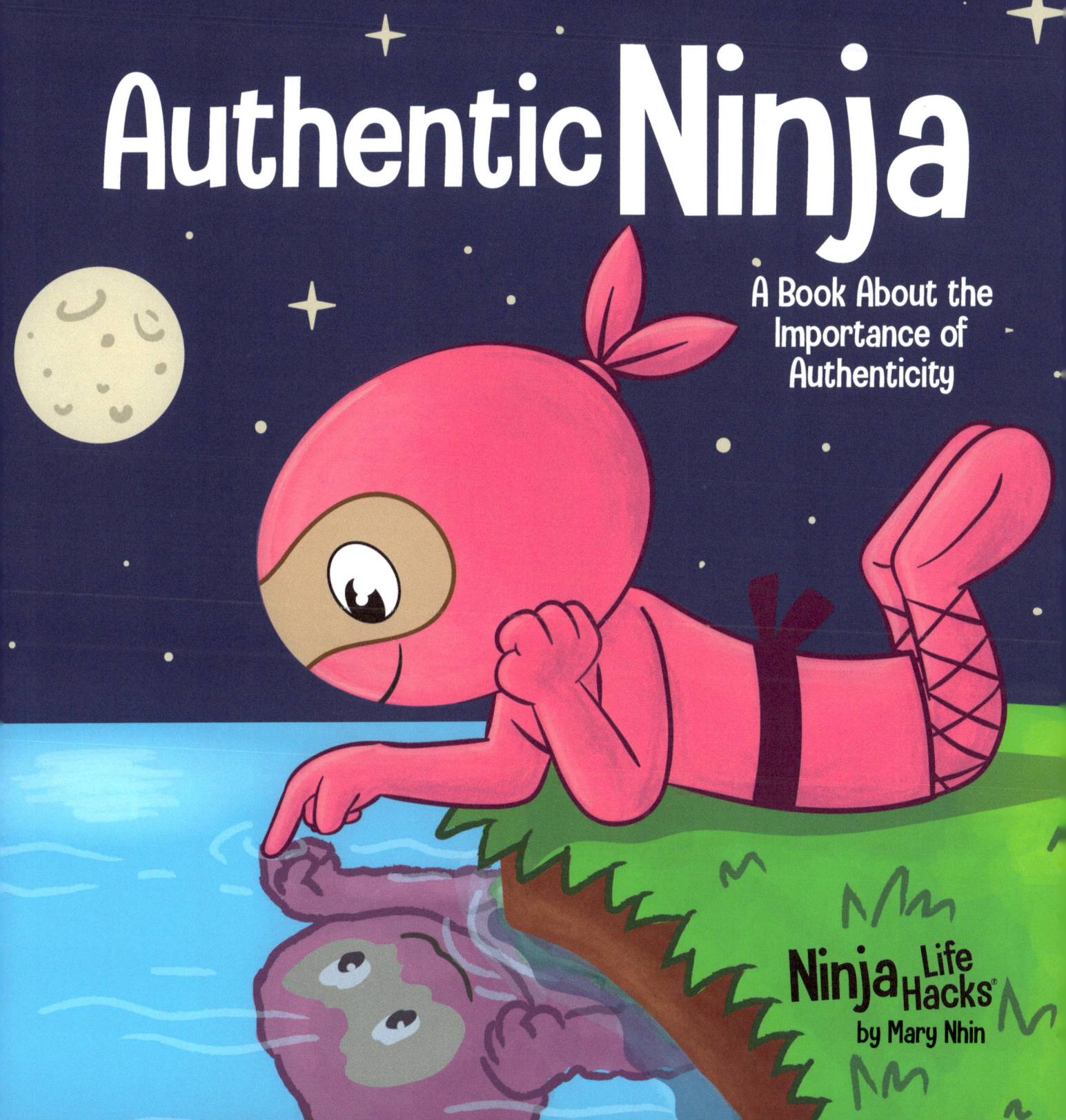

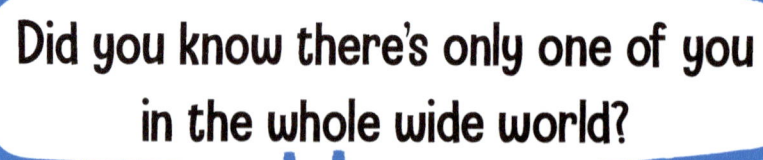

When my friend chose mint as her favorite flavor, I chose mint, too, even though my favorite flavor was berry.

L is for Listen to Your Heart. To stay authentic, you want to tune in to the voice inside you and follow what makes you truly happy, just like a compass pointing north! The voice inside you guides you based on your values.

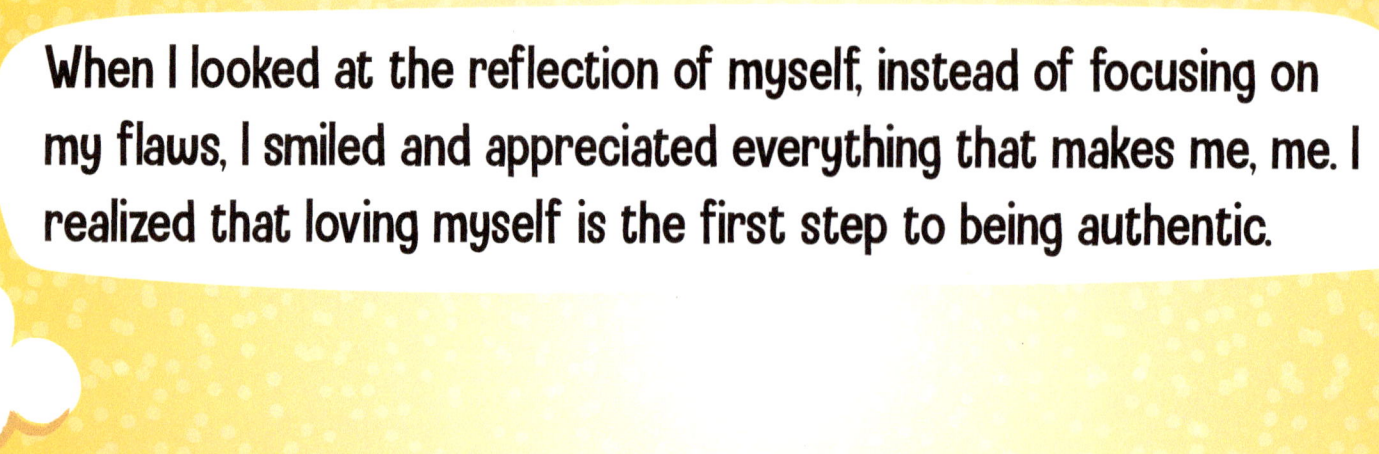

When I looked at the reflection of myself, instead of focusing on my flaws, I smiled and appreciated everything that makes me, me. I realized that loving myself is the first step to being authentic.

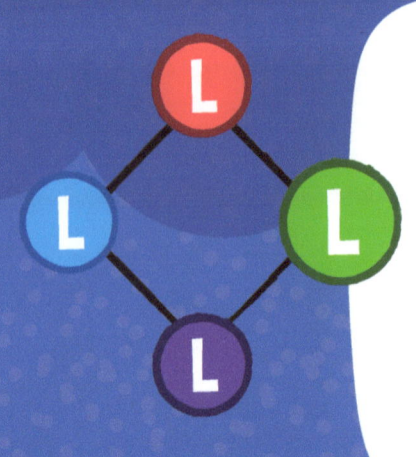

L is for Live Your Truth. Being authentic means staying true to your values and beliefs, even when faced with challenges. Don't let others define who you are and don't give into peer pressure.

Peer pressure is when someone tries to make you do something you're not comfortable with. It's okay to stand your ground.

L is for **Lean on Others**. Being authentic means sharing your true self with others and leaning on them for support when you need it.

As I journeyed along the path, I realized that it's okay to ask for help and reach out to my friends when I'm feeling down or needing help. They're always there to lift me up and support me.

When we reached the spot, I discovered a treasure chest filled with sparkling jewels. Each jewel represented a moment where I embraced authenticity and stayed true to myself.

From that day on, I made a promise to always...

And do you know what? You can be authentic too!

Remembering the magic of the 4 Ls could be your secret weapon in developing authenticity!

In a world with so much to do and see,
There's someone I adore, and that is me!
With a twinkle in my eye and a skip in my feet,
I dance to the rhythm of my own beat.

Some days I'm full of cheer,
Other days, there are things I fear.
I speak my truth and sing a song,
In this world, I do belong!

Continue the learning with the Authentic Ninja lesson plans which include superpower skills practice, STEM activity, craft, and more!

 @marynhin @officialninjalifehacks
#NinjaLifeHacks

 Ninja Life Hacks

 Mary Nhin   Ninja Life Hacks

 @officialninjalifehacks

www.ingramcontent.com/pod-product-compliance
Lightning Source LLC
Chambersburg PA
CBHW041521070526
44585CB00002B/30